The
Tiara
Club

✦ AT SILVER TOWERS ✦

The Tiara Club

Princess Charlotte *and the* Birthday Ball

Princess Katie *and the* Silver Pony

Princess Daisy *and the* Dazzling Dragon

Princess Sophia *and the* Sparkling Surprise

Princess Alice *and the* Magical Mirror

Princess Emily *and the* Substitute Fairy

The Tiara Club at Silver Towers

Princess Charlotte *and the* Enchanted Rose

Princess Katie *and the* Mixed-up Potion

Princess Daisy *and the* Magical Merry-Go-Round

Princess Alice *and the* Glass Slipper

Princess Emily *and the* Wishing Star

VIVIAN FRENCH

The Tiara Club

✦ AT SILVER TOWERS ✦

Princess Sophia
AND THE
Prince's Party

ILLUSTRATED BY SARAH GIBB

KATHERINE TEGEN BOOKS
HarperTrophy®
An Imprint of HarperCollins*Publishers*

The Tiara Club at Silver Towers: Princess Sophia and the
Prince's Party
Text copyright © 2007 by Vivian French
Illustrations copyright © 2007 by Sarah Gibb

Library of Congress Cataloging-in-Publication Data
French, Vivian.
Princess Sophia and the prince's party / by Vivian French ;
illustrated by Sarah Gibb. — 1st U.S. ed.
   p.   cm. — (Tiara Club at Silver Towers)
"Katherine Tegen books."
Summary: Princess Sophia encourages a shy prince to dance
with her at the Princes' Academy ball.
ISBN: 978-0-06-112449-5
   [1. Princesses—Fiction. 2. Dance—Fiction. 3. Balls (Par-
ties)—Fiction.] I. Gibb, Sarah, ill. II. Title.
PZ7.F88917Prp 2007   2007011863
[Fic]—dc22   CIP
                                                                      AC

Typography by Amy Ryan
❖
First U.S. edition, 2007

For Princess Catriona of Trinity,
with love, xx
—V.F.

For Lucy, a friend forever
—S.G.

The Royal Palace Academy
for the Preparation of Perfect Princesses
(Known to our students as "The Princess Academy")

OUR SCHOOL MOTTO:
A Perfect Princess always thinks of others before herself,
and is kind, caring, and truthful.

Silver Towers offers a complete education for Tiara Club princesses with emphasis on selected outings. The curriculum includes:

Fans and Curtseys

A visit to Witch Windlespin
(Royal herbalist, healer, and maker of magic potions)

Problem Prime Ministers

A visit to the Museum of Royal Life
(Students will be well protected from the Poisoned Apple)

Our principal, Queen Samantha Joy, is present at all times, and students are in the excellent care of the school Fairy Godmother, Fairy Angora.

OUR RESIDENT STAFF & VISITING EXPERTS INCLUDE:

LADY ALBINA MacSPLINTER *(School Secretary)*
CROWN PRINCE DANDINO *(Field Trips)*
QUEEN MOTHER MATILDA *(Etiquette, Posture, and Poise)*
FAIRY G. *(Head Fairy Godmother)*

We award tiara points to encourage our
Tiara Club princesses toward the next level.
All princesses who win enough points at Silver
Towers will attend the Silver Ball, where they
will be presented with their Silver Sashes.

Silver Sash Tiara Club princesses are invited
to return to Ruby Mansions, our exclusive
residence for Perfect Princesses, where they may
continue their education at a higher level.

PLEASE NOTE:
Princesses are expected to arrive
at the Academy with a *minimum* of:

TWENTY BALL GOWNS
*(with all necessary hoops,
petticoats, etc.)*

TWELVE DAY-DRESSES

SEVEN GOWNS
*suitable for garden parties
and other special daytime
occasions*

TWELVE TIARAS

DANCING SHOES
five pairs

VELVET SLIPPERS
three pairs

RIDING BOOTS
two pairs

*Cloaks, muffs, stoles, gloves,
and other essential
accessories, as required*

Hello! I'm Princess Sophia, and I'm a Tiara Club Princess here at Silver Towers, just like you! And I'm so glad you're here with us.

I think you know my friends who share the Silver Rose Room with me. There's Alice, and Daisy, and Katie and Charlotte and Emily, and I just know that if we get enough tiara points to earn our Silver Sashes and go on to Ruby Mansions, we'll still be the very best friends ever.

We're not too friendly with Princess Diamonde and her twin sister, Gruella, though. They just love showing off and being mean.

Chapter One

It was Wednesday, and we were late getting up. Princess Katie was still in her pajamas and Princess Alice was only half dressed when the last bell rang for breakfast. Princess Charlotte dropped her hairbrush and looked horrified.

"Oh no!" she said. "Lady Albina's going to be furious. We'll get a million minus tiara points!"

Lady Albina is the school secretary, and she's usually floating around at breakfast time. She only smiles when Queen Samantha Joy is around, and she's always scolding us for not being Perfect Princesses, and handing out minus tiara points.

Princess Emily groaned. "I've already got three this week," she said. "I forgot to hand in my Ideal Banquet Arrangements to Lady Victoria, and she was in a bad mood."

"But we did get five tiara points each for knowing how to flutter a fan while curtseying," I said.

"You mean *you* did," Katie said

as she scrambled into her clothes. "I only got two."

Princess Daisy sighed. "Me too."

"Never mind about fans," Charlotte interrupted. "Let's go!"

We hurried down the stairs, hoping we might be able to sneak in without being seen.

But Lady Albina was standing outside the dining hall tacking a notice on the board. She frowned at us as we sank into our most apologetic curtseys.

"I'm so sorry we're late, Lady Albina," I said.

Lady Albina looked at her watch in a serious manner. "You are very

late indeed, Princess Sophia," she snapped. "Such behavior is intolerable! Please report to Queen Samantha Joy immediately after breakfast, and I will not be at all surprised if she forbids you to attend Prince Maurice's party." Then she sniffed loudly and stalked away with her nose in the air.

We stared at one another. Finally Emily asked, "Who's Prince Maurice? And why would he ask us to his party?"

Alice shook her head. "I don't know. My big sister's never said anything about a Prince Maurice."

Charlotte sighed. "I hope we can

go. It's been forever since we've been to a party."

Daisy was looking worried. "Do you think Queen Samantha Joy will be very mad at us?"

"We'd better have breakfast and

find out," Katie said, and we followed her into the dining hall.

Of course, the only seats left were next to the terrible twins, Princess Diamonde and Princess Gruella, and Diamonde looked *so* superior as we sat down.

"Don't any of you know that

Perfect Princesses are supposed to be on time for their appointments?" she asked.

We ignored her, and Emily turned to Gruella. "Do you know anything about a party?" she asked. "Prince Maurice's party?"

Gruella shook her head, and

Diamonde rolled her eyes at us.

"Typical." She sneered and said, "Of course one of the Silver Rose Roomers would pretend she knows something before the rest of us!"

Emily turned red and bit her lip. I jumped up and glared at Diamonde.

"That's so unfair!" I said. "Lady Albina told us." As I spoke, I suddenly remembered.

Lady Albina had been putting up a notice when we saw her. I was so sure it was about the party that I went to check and walked straight into our principal, Queen Samantha Joy.

Chapter Two

Queen Samantha Joy gave me a surprised stare.

"Would you mind telling me why you're not in the dining hall, Princess Sophia?" she asked.

"Please forgive me, Your Majesty," I stammered, and I curtsied right down to the ground. "I was going to look at the bulletin board."

Our principal turned to the board and inspected it. "There is nothing here to attract such enthusiastic interest," she told me. "Only a note to say that from now on, any princess who is late for breakfast will be given five minus tiara points. I trust, Princess Sophia, that *you* were not late this morning?"

I didn't know what to say. I hung my head and stared at the floor. "Yes, Your Majesty," I whispered. "Lady Albina said we were to report to you after breakfast."

Queen Samantha Joy frowned.

"This is *not* the way I expect my princesses to behave," she said. "Do you think it is the proper way to behave, Princess Sophia?"

My eyes filled with tears.

The one thing I've always wanted more than anything else in the whole wide world is to be a Perfect Princess and I'd totally let myself down. All I could think of to say was, "I'm very, very sorry, Your Majesty."

"I should hope so," the principal said. "And now, you'd better come with me. I have an announcement to make."

She swept into the dining hall, and I hurried after her.

I could see my friends looking anxious as I slid into my seat, but I couldn't tell them what had happened because Queen Samantha Joy was already speaking.

"Princesses! My nephew, Prince Maurice of Charmover, has graduated from the Royal Palace Academy for the Preparation of Perfect Princes with nine hundred and ninety-five crown points out of a possible one thousand. The Academy would like to celebrate his remarkable achievement, and

the principal, King Ferdinand, has invited every one of you to a ball to be held next Saturday evening." Queen Samantha Joy stopped and smiled. "And I've arranged for extra dancing lessons so the princesses from Silver Towers will be the belles of the ball!"

It was so quiet you could have

heard a pin drop. Really! And then everybody began to talk at once, until our principal raised her hand.

"I'm glad you're so excited," she said. "Of course, it goes without saying that I expect only the best behavior from my girls. Which reminds me." She turned and looked sternly at me. "Princess Sophia, tell me truthfully: Do you think you deserve to go to Prince Maurice's party?"

I didn't know what to say. I felt *awful*! Of course I was dying to go, but I wanted to win my Silver Sash and go on to Ruby Mansions even more. I took a deep breath and curtsied again.

"Your Majesty," I said, "I'm very, very sorry. And I don't know if I deserve to go to the party." I swallowed hard. "But whatever you decide, I do promise to try to behave better in the future."

Queen Samantha Joy looked thoughtful, but before she could say anything, Emily stood up.

"Please, Your Majesty," she said, "if Sophia can't go, then I shouldn't be allowed to go either."

"Me neither," Alice said, and she, Charlotte, Katie, and Daisy stood up as well.

"We were *all* late for breakfast, Your Majesty," Katie explained.

"I see." Queen Samantha Joy gave a little chuckle. "Well, perhaps Princess Sophia *should* go to the party. Any princess who inspires such loyalty in her friends must be worthy of a second chance."

"Thank you, Your Majesty," I said. "Oh, thank you!"

Our principal nodded at me. "Just remember, Princess Sophia, no third chances!" And she walked away.

I sank into my chair. "Thank you all so much," I said to my friends. "That was so nice of you!"

"But we couldn't have gone without you," Emily said.

"Silver Rose Roomers forever!"
Katie cheered.

Diamonde sniffed. "Well," she said, "if Queen Samantha Joy had asked me, I'd have said none of you deserved to go!" And she flounced out of the dining hall.

Alice grinned. "Never mind her. What are we going to wear?"

Chapter Three

We were still trying to decide when
the five-minute warning bell rang
for our first class. We hurried off
to our Wednesday lesson on
Problematic Prime Ministers, but
halfway up the stairs we met
Princess Eglantine coming down

with Princess Nancy.

"All classes are canceled," she said happily. "We've got Dance instead and we've got to go to the Silver Ballroom."

"Hurrah!" Charlotte did a twirl on the stairs. "Who's teaching Dance class?"

Nancy grinned. "We think it might be Fairy Angora, but we're not sure."

"Oh, double hurrah!" Alice said, and we all positively bounced down the stairs and made our way to the ballroom. Fairy Angora is our school Fairy Godmother, and she's just wonderful, even if she's a bit scatterbrained at times.

But it wasn't Fairy Angora waiting for us. It was Lady Albina, and my heart sank as I saw her. I had this terrible feeling that I was going to get in trouble again and I'd end up not being allowed to go to Prince Maurice's party.

Lady Albina gave me such an icy look when she saw me, but she didn't say anything. She sailed across the room and signaled to the Silver Towers Musicians. They began to play a really bouncy sort of tune; it made my feet twitch just hearing it!

Lady Albina frowned at them. "Stop that at once!" she ordered, and she sounded so rude. "We need something much slower."

I saw the conductor give the musicians the teeniest of winks, and they began to play the gloomiest music ever. *Dah . . . dah . . . dah . . . ,* it went.

It was so hard not to laugh. I had

to pretend I was blowing my nose, because I knew that if I did laugh, Lady Albina would be furious. Alice, Emily, and Katie turned their giggles into coughs, but Daisy and Charlotte didn't manage nearly so well.

"Princess Daisy! Princess Charlotte! I do *not* see anything to laugh about!" Lady Albina snapped. "Please try to behave properly!"

"Yes, Lady Albina," Charlotte said, and Daisy curtsied.

Lady Albina glared at the musicians. "Please play faster!"

The musicians burst into a wonderfully catchy polka and at

once every princess seized a partner and began to bound around the room.

"No no no *no!*" Lady Albina clapped her hands to stop us. "You have been invited to the Princes' Academy, and this ridiculous hopping and skipping is quite unsuitable. You must sit calmly until a prince invites you to dance, and then you will either waltz or foxtrot as appropriate. Princess Daisy, please come here. You too, Princess Sophia. I will teach you the basic steps, and I expect everyone to pay close attention. Musicians, a slow tempo waltz, *if* you please!"

The next hour was awful! Lady Albina made me dance the boy's steps, so I was going forward. Daisy did the girl's steps, so she was going backward. Lady Albina kept saying,

"One two *three*, one two *three!*" when I absolutely knew the music was going *one* two three, *one* two three, and every single princess was getting more and more confused. They were trying to copy what

Lady Albina told Daisy and me to do, but as we kept getting it wrong they did too. It was really awful.

Lady Albina got more and more annoyed, and her instructions made less and less sense. I thought she was going to explode as I stepped on poor Daisy's toes for about the millionth time, but luckily the bell rang for the end of the lesson, and she stormed out.

We felt really gloomy as we trailed out of the ballroom. We'd always loved dancing before, but somehow Lady Albina made it seem so difficult. And it didn't get much better on Thursday or Friday.

"I think my feet are getting bigger."
I sighed as we were dismissed from
our last class.

"It wasn't quite so bad today,"
Charlotte said. "And it honestly

isn't your fault—Lady Albina's completely hopeless at telling us what to do."

Gruella snickered. "Lady Albina said you made elephants look graceful."

"Don't listen to her." Alice put her arm through mine. "Let's go and try on our dresses for tomorrow."

Chapter Four

Can you keep a secret?

Yes. I know you can.

I really, really hate being bad at things. Is that terrible of me? Well, it's true.

I woke up really early on the morning of Prince Maurice's party because I was so worried. I don't want to boast, but I'd always been one of the best at dancing in Fairy Angora's classes, but Lady Albina had made me feel as if I could never dance again. I looked across at my beautiful ball gown and my shoes and my fan. And instead of feeling excited, I felt sick.

"Sophia? Are you OK?" Daisy was sitting up in bed.

"I think so," I said.

Alice yawned. "It'll be fun to see the Princes' Academy," she said.

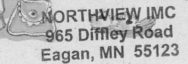

"What do you think the princes will be like?"

"Most boys are boring." Emily was awake too. "My brothers certainly are."

"Diamonde thinks Prince Maurice will sweep her off her feet and dance with her until midnight," Charlotte said with a giggle. "But Gruella thinks he'll choose *her*. I heard them arguing about it!"

Katie threw back her covers. "He must be really old," she pointed out. "He won't notice any of us. Come on, let's get up!"

By the time the coaches came to bring us to the party, I was feeling a bit better. After all, I was with all my best friends, even if my dancing was hopeless. And it *was* nice to have a chance to wear my very best ball gown.

As the coach drew up at the

front door of the Princes' Academy, Katie gave us a thumbs-up. It wasn't a very princessy thing to do, but it made us laugh.

The princes' ballroom was wonderful! The walls were a rich red, and the ceiling was glittering gold. There were lots of sparkling chandeliers, and down one side of the room was a row of golden pillars. Beyond them I could see tables piled with food and lots of comfy sofas, but the ballroom seemed very empty. At one end, a group of princes was huddled together looking awkward, and at the other, a row of princesses was sitting stiffly on little golden chairs.

"Oops!" Alice whispered in my ear. "It doesn't look very fun!"

We made our way to the chairs and sat down.

"Maybe we'll sit here all evening," Emily said, but at that moment, there was a fanfare of trumpets. A king dressed in the most splendid robes came marching in, and beside him was Queen Samantha Joy, looking magnificent.

"No one is dancing? We can't have that!" the king boomed. "Start the music! Everyone dance! Come along, boys! Lots of princesses to dance with here. Choose a partner, and have fun!"

At once, the musicians burst into a waltz.

None of the princes moved.

"Hurry up!" the king barked at

them. "This is a *ball*. You're supposed to dance!"

The princes shifted around, and
at last a tall, very handsome prince
walked toward us.

"I bet that's Prince Maurice,"

Charlotte said. "Look at Diamonde and Gruella!"

The twin princesses were both sitting straight up, fluttering their fans madly, and smiling huge smiles, but the prince didn't seem

to notice them. He came straight
toward me and bowed.

"May I have the honor of this
dance, Your Highness?" he asked.

I stood up. The prince grabbed
my hand and swung me onto the

floor, and I was waltzing.

Only I wasn't, because every-thing Lady Albina had said sud-denly flooded into my head, and my feet felt huge. Instead of danc-ing backward, I stepped forward. At once I knew that was so wrong, so I tried to change, stepped on my own toes, wobbled, staggered, and fell over!

Chapter Five

I don't think I've ever been so embarrassed! My face was burning red as I struggled to my feet, and I ran out. Behind me I heard the tall prince absolutely howling with laughter, and I just wanted to die. I dashed between the pillars and hid behind a sofa in a corner. I shut my eyes, flapped my fan to cool my face, and thought, *I won't cry! I won't cry! Perfect Princesses don't feel sorry for themselves,* but it was so hard.

And then I heard a noise. A tiny cough.

I opened my eyes and peered over the arm of the sofa. A very ordinary-looking prince with scruffy hair was standing on the other side holding a glass of water and a white tissue. When he saw me looking, he bowed very politely.

"It's quite all right to cry, you know," he said, and he smiled the sweetest smile. "It's terrible when people laugh at you. People often laugh at me, and I can never get used to it. Would you like a tissue? Or would you prefer the water?"

I couldn't help staring at him.

He was about my height, so I thought he must be quite young. He wasn't at all like what I'd expected a prince to be, but he was so nice I couldn't help smiling back.

"The water, please," I said.

"Good choice," the prince said. "I knew as soon as I saw you that you were a Perfect Princess."

I shook my head. "Prince Maurice doesn't think so," I said.

A strange expression flitted across the scruffy-haired prince's face. "Prince Maurice?" he asked.

"He asked me to dance, and I fell over," I explained. "He couldn't stop laughing!"

"Oh, yes. Yes, I saw that," the prince said. He hesitated and continued. "Don't you think that was rather mean of him?"

"I suppose it was," I said slowly.

"But I don't know anything about princes and how they should behave."

The prince shook his head. "No Perfect Prince should ever laugh at the misfortunes of others! Although they laughed at me all the time in Dance class. They made me dance the girl's steps, you see, because I'm small." He sighed. "That's why I'm hiding here. I got five minus crown points, and I won't dare ask anyone to dance."

I began to giggle. "But that's what happened to *me*!" I said. "Only the other way around, of course." And then an amazing idea popped into my head, and before I could stop myself, I said, "Why don't we dance together? It won't matter at all if we get it wrong—we're both used to it!"

The scruffy-haired prince's eyes shone, and he smiled a huge smile.

"Would you really dance with me?" he asked.

"Of course!" I said, and at that exact moment the musicians burst into the hoppiest, skippiest polka you've ever heard. "Come on!" I said, and we rushed onto the dance floor.

Around and around we danced, and as we passed my friends, Katie grabbed Charlotte, and Emily caught Daisy's hand, and they all whizzed after us. And then I saw Alice twirling around and around with a prince! It was so much fun.

And then the music stopped, and there was the loudest cheer. It was so loud it made the chandeliers shake! And I suddenly realized that *the cheer was for me and the scruffy-haired prince*!

Queen Samantha Joy sailed onto the dance floor. Her eyes were twinkling.

"I wish to extend my congratulations to Princess Sophia, the first princess ever to persuade my beloved nephew, Prince Maurice, to dance."

I stared at the scruffy-haired prince. *He* was Prince Maurice!

"And very fine dancers they both

are!" the king agreed as he strode up. "So fine, indeed, that I have to award Prince Maurice his last five crown points, so he now has one thousand."

And everybody burst into more wild cheering until Prince Maurice stepped forward.

"I'd just like to say," he began,

"that the only reason I'm dancing is because I've found the Perfect Princess to dance with!" He turned to me and bowed, and as he stood up, he winked a cheerful wink. "And now that I've found my dancing feet, I shall ask Princess Sophia to be my partner in the Princes' Academy Celebration Waltz."

Chapter Six

The rest of the evening was so fabulous. We Rose Roomers danced with one another, and we danced with the princes, and once I even danced with the king! Luckily it was a country dance, so I didn't

have to worry about going forward
or backward.

And when the time came to go
home, we collapsed into the coach
feeling so happy.

Just as the coachman was about
to shake his reins, the coach door

opened and Queen Samantha Joy smiled in at us.

"I wanted to say how proud I am of you, my dears," she said. She leaned across and took my hand. "You did so well, Princess Sophia. Prince Maurice was quite right.

You are indeed a Perfect Princess, and you and your friends from the Silver Rose Room truly deserve to be the belles of the ball!" Then she blew us a kiss and closed the coach door.

That night, I dreamed wonderful dreams of floating in a silver ballroom with all my friends.

And I just know you were there too.

Princess Emily
∽ AND THE ∽
Wishing Star

Hi! This is Princess Emily saying
hello and I'm so pleased you're
here with us at Silver Towers.
Charlotte, Katie, Daisy, Alice,
Sophia, and I have such a good
time . . . except when horrid Princess Diamonde
and her twin sister, Gruella, try to spoil
everything, of course.

We'd been keeping our fingers crossed
for ages that we'd gotten enough tiara
points to win our Silver Sashes, but suddenly
it was nearly time for the Silver Ball. And
we began to panic—especially me!

You are cordially invited
to the Royal Princess Academy:

Follow the adventures of your special princess friends
as they try to earn enough points to join the Tiara Club.

Katherine Tegen Books
An Imprint of HarperCollinsPublishers